"An imaginative way to teach everyone about the life-saving work of rescue dogs and about the bond between handler and dog."

Dan Hourihan, President
National Association for Search and Rescue

"There is perhaps no more rewarding task for a police officer than finding a lost child. *Faith in Fay* captures all the drama, the suspense, the urgency, and the reward of these missions. It's a great story, and a great way to learn about canine rescue teams."

William J. Johnson, Executive Director
National Association of Police Organizations, Inc.

"*Faith in Fay* is a marvelous story for adults to read to children and for young readers to read themselves. The lessons taught through the life-saving work of rescue dogs and the bond between handler and dog are inspirational and will captivate the attention of young readers everywhere. As a classroom teacher, I see many ways to use this story with classroom lessons and student learning. I hope this is only the first of Fay's adventures."

Becky Felts, President
OEA (Oklahoma Office of the National Education Association)

"*Faith in Fay* inspires us to trust the dog to do what we cannot. Fay's handler carefully nurtured her natural abilities with positive reinforcement. A remarkable story about a remarkable dog."

Tulsa SPCA

"*Faith in Fay* is a wonderful story that explores the human-animal bond between a dog and her owner as they work as a team to serve humankind through Search and Rescue (SAR). Fay embodies the essence of the working nature of the Border Collie breed, how loyal, intelligent, and "biddable" the dogs are, and also how much activity they require to adequately use their talents and keep them mentally challenged. An endearing read for children and adults alike."

Border Collie Society of America

"All firefighters love to work directly with children and *Faith in Fay* dovetails with canine rescue. Reading to children such a success story only reinforces these principles."

Chris Bain, EFO, Executive Director
Oklahoma State Firefighters Association

Faith in Fay
Series
Adventures of a Rescue Dog

the
Lost Child

Adventures of a Rescue Dog

the
Lost Child

Sherri Watson and Paula Abney

Brown Books Publishing Group
Dallas, Texas

Faith in Fay: Adventures of a Rescue Dog
The Lost Child

© 2009 Sherri Watson and Paula Abney

Written by Sherri Watson and Paula Abney.
Illustrated by Claire Howard.

Manufactured in the United States of America.

For information, please contact:

Brown Books Publishing Group
16200 North Dallas Parkway, Suite 170
Dallas, Texas 75248
www.brownbooks.com
972-248-9500

A New Era in Publishing™

ISBN-13: 978-1-934812-49-5
ISBN-10: 1-934812-49-8
LCCN: 2009930382

Author contact information:

Sherri Watson or Paula Abney
www.faithinfay.com

This book is dedicated to Sherri's devoted husband and friend, Gary Watson, and to his companions, Sam and Lexi—the parents of Fay—all lost to us, but together somewhere in a better place. Your faithful loyalty and joy for life affected everyone around you. The legacies of you three will live on through this book, as your memories live on in our hearts.

Acknowledgments

We never would have believed when this adventure began that we would end up here. The legacy of memories from years ago has been passed forward and continues to grow. Our dream was to educate the public in search and rescue while continuing the legend of a great team: Gary and the Border collie duo, Sam and Lexi. There are many people whom we want to thank for helping us to move this legacy forward.

We thank God for His patience, love, strength, and continued guidance in our lives.

Thank you to our children for their unconditional love and patience.

Thanks to Claire for the art and illustrations.

Also to Jim Abney for his support and patience while we pursued our dreams.

And to our families and friends. Without their love and support, this book would have never happened.

Thank you to Brown Books Publishing Group and our publishing team, especially Milli Brown; Kathryn Grant;

Dr. Janet Harris; Nina Romberg; Bill Young; Jessica Kinkel; Jennifer Allen, and Rachel Felts for their patience, understanding, and incredible ability to help us place on paper what has been in our hearts. And thanks to Cindy Birne and Cathy Williams, the awesome PR team. Additionally, Fay wants to thank Milli for the treats, Kathryn for the Vienna sausages, and the rest of the team for the hugs and entertainment.

Thank you to all of the individuals who participate in the training of search and rescue dogs and their handlers. Also to all the search and rescue groups and people who continue to volunteer their time: keep up the good work.

We have to give a big WOW to Fay's Faithful Friends; thanks for the donations and contributions. We are here because of your help.

Thank you to Redstone Visual for providing us with your time and energy without ever wanting anything in return.

We would like to thank Steve Carichoff for his love and patience. He has been a silent, unselfish giver of love and support.

Most of all, we want to thank our little dog sister, Fay, for the adventure of a lifetime.

We love all of you and pray you continue to be in our adventures now and the ones that lie ahead. Hang on—this ride is just beginning!

Foreword

Dear Sherri,

What a fun and quick read! I had tears in my eyes several times. More importantly, you, Paula, and Fay have inspired me. I recently found my creative side and began oil painting, a hobby I enjoy very much for the feeling of accomplishment upon completing a work of art that has been dancing around in my head. I will likely continue painting as long as I'm able to hold a brush, but my first love is writing.

For some time, I've been thinking about writing a book—in particular, a children's book. Now, thanks to the inspiration I found in *Faith in Fay*, I may just do it. I thoroughly enjoyed this intriguing, educational story. Chock-full of important lessons, this is an adventure of substance, suspense, and fun that is sure to keep young readers turning pages. Fay will tug at your heartstrings. This may be the perfect children's book. Your team has done a good job. I expect to see many more of Fay's adventures.

Sincerely,
Brad Henry
Governor, State of Oklahoma

Chapter

One

"Are you ready to work?"

Fay pricked up her ears at the familiar phrase and cocked her head to one side. Excitement gleamed in her brown eyes.

A call had come in for our help and we'd hit the road. A little girl named Maddi was lost. Fay's keen sense of smell was needed to find her.

Fay came from a long line of Border collies who were bred to herd cattle and buffalo on an Oklahoma ranch. Now she worked as a search and rescue dog. She was

small, but she made up the difference in smarts, strength, and focus. She had glossy black fur and white markings on her throat, chest, feet, and the tip of her long tail.

My name is Tess Malone, but in search and rescue, I'm mostly known as Fay's handler. I interpret Fay's body language for authorities during a missing person search. I take care of Fay's food, water, and shelter. I also transport her to searches.

Best of all, Fay and I are best friends and are as close as sisters. We share our lives. Good and bad. Work and play. We do it all together.

As a rescue team, we are part of a huge nationwide network of volunteer emergency responders. We belong to a local search and rescue group; law enforcement agencies and fire departments call us to search for missing people.

At the rescue scene, I parked under a shade tree and sat a moment in my SUV with its magnetic Search & Rescue signs on the doors. I surveyed the area. Open fields and woods surrounded us. There were no nearby houses or rushing cars on busy roads. Several police cars blocked the driveway to a two-story, white farmhouse with a green roof. Ancient oak trees cast shadows over the front lawn. A picket fence enclosed a large backyard. People clustered in groups, talking, looking, and gesturing.

A child's safety depended on Fay's ability to track and my ability to interpret her actions. I took a deep breath to slow my racing heart. I needed to be calm and collected to do my job well.

Fay poked the back of my arm with her cold nose. She was eager too. I turned around to look into her intelligent eyes. She appeared alert. She knew she was on the job. She sat waiting in what she considered her seat in our vehicle. I kept the seat behind me folded down and she sat in the one behind the front passenger seat. She liked to lap water from her cup holder with a dog bowl in it. Keeping a search dog hydrated is a top priority.

I reached back and ruffled her thick, black fur. She licked my arm, tasting my sunscreen. She loved lotion of all kinds.

"Fay, I'll get started and then be back for you."

She thumped her tail enthusiastically against the seat in acknowledgment. Every inch of her was taut, ready to go to work.

I lowered all the SUV's windows and hung a battery-operated fan in the passenger side so Fay would stay fairly cool. I stepped out into hot, muggy air and hoped my clothes wouldn't be too warm. I wore standard handler's gear: jeans, hiking boots, and a long-sleeved shirt emblazoned with Search & Rescue on the back. I keep my unruly dark hair cut short for convenience on the job. Plus, I look more like Fay.

I work out in a gym to stay strong enough to handle rescue work. I jog to maintain stamina for the long searches through rough country. And I play Frisbee with Fay to keep us both in shape. We also train once a week to be ready for a search and rescue call.

After I zipped open my search bag, I pulled out my scent article kit that held ziplock bags, sterile gauze pads, sterile latex gloves, and a permanent marker.

When Fay and I start a search, we can never be sure of the outcome. But no matter how long it lasts or what it takes, we do our best to get the job done right. Lives depend on our actions.

I carried my scent kit as I walked over to Bowen, the Incident Commander. We'd worked with him before. He was experienced, plus cool and calm. As I.C., he was responsible for sending search teams to specific areas, providing food and water for volunteers, and keeping up communications. He was good at his job.

"Tess, glad to see you," Bowen boomed, his voice as big as his burly body.

Smiling, I shook his gnarled hand. I felt a strong sense of confidence setting out with such an excellent I.C. in charge. "Good to see you too."

"Where's my favorite girl?"

"Fay's in the car. I bet she's howling her head off if she knows you're here."

He chuckled. "I like her too."

"I'll bring her by to see you later."

"Do that. For now, if you're ready, we've got someone at the house to help you. He'll be flanking for you."

"Thanks. I'll go on up and get to work." I started toward the house.

"And Tess."

I turned back.

"Find that little girl before it's too late."

"We'll do our best."

"Let's hope a stranger didn't take her from the front yard. Her scent will be harder to follow, maybe impossible."

I nodded. "Let's get Fay on the job."

"Good luck."

Chapter

Two

I felt tension all around me as I walked up to the house. People watched me with hope and fear on their faces. They had good reason for both emotions. Hope that Fay's amazing sense of smell could find Maddi. And fear that too much was working against us. At six in the evening, night was coming on. The temperature was at least a hundred degrees. And a storm was brewing. Any one of those conditions made search and rescue harder, but all three made it a real challenge. Worse, how could a little girl survive it all?

I nodded as I passed them, squaring my shoulders and hardening my resolve for the task ahead. I stepped up onto the wide front porch. Normally, it would be a cozy family place to sit together on the white wicker furniture with green plush cushions. I could imagine a little girl on the wooden swing, pushing back and forth, happily chattering. All was empty now. And silent.

I pulled open the screen door and stepped inside. I took a deep breath. It's always difficult to meet the family and friends. They are in great emotional pain. Emotion can get in the way of doing a good job, so I focus on my work.

My eyes adjusted to the dim light in the foyer. People clustered in groups, speaking softly and urgently. Their worry was in sharp contrast to the home's comfortable interior. Blue flower wallpaper, antique furniture, and delicate knickknacks suited the farmhouse.

A tall, lanky fireman walked over and held out his hand. He had dark hair and eyes. He wore a crisp uniform. "I'm Noah, your flanker. I'll be with you every step of the way."

"Good to meet you." I shook his hand. "I'm Tess, Fay's handler."

"Glad you're here. What do you need?"

"I'd like to talk with the parents."

"You got it." Noah turned and waved over a man and a woman. "These are Maddi's parents, Ben and Tamara James."

Maddi's dad was medium height with curly, light-brown hair and warm brown eyes that were shaded with worry and frustration. Her mom was small with straight blond hair and large blue eyes that were red-rimmed from crying.

"Thank you for coming," Tamara said.

"I wish we were here under better circumstances." I tried to ease the situation with kind words.

"We're just glad you're here," Ben said.

"We're worried sick about Maddi." Tamara blinked away tears.

"Let me reassure you," I said. "Fay is good at this. She's also very experienced. We'll do our best to find your daughter." My heart went out to the young couple. They stood stiffly together as if bracing against a strong wind. I'd do my best to save their child.

"Thank you for your help," Ben said. "What can we do?"

"Please tell me about Maddi."

"She's smart and beautiful." Tamara said. "Six years old. A bundle of energy with blond hair and blue eyes."

"What is she wearing?"

"A pink tank top, denim shorts, and white tennis shoes that flash with red lights when she walks," Tamara said.

"Tell me about the soles of the shoes."

"They're her favorites, but they're so worn there's little tread left," Tamara said.

"It doesn't matter to Fay. I just need to know in case we do find footprints to verify they are Maddi's. Any other features?"

Tamara looked at Ben and then nodded. "Yes. There's a large flower on the sole and a small flower on the heel."

"Good. That helps a lot. Now, how did she get lost?"

"We were in the backyard." Tamara twisted her hands together. "I was glancing through a magazine while she played with her cat. Sasha is a long-haired tabby."

I nodded to encourage her story.

"The phone rang and I stepped inside to answer it." Tamara took a deep, calming breath. "When I came back, Maddi was gone. Sasha too."

"Then what?"

"I searched for half an hour all around the yard, front and back, and into the pasture. Nothing. I called my husband and the police."

"After they came, what did you do?"

"We all looked again, called out, but still no Maddi or Sasha." Tamara clutched her husband's hand.

Ben cleared his throat. "What happened, we think, is that Maddi followed Sasha out the back gate. It was unlatched and open."

"We didn't even realize Maddi could reach or work the latch on the gate," Tamara said. "We never dreamed she could push it open through the heavy grass."

"I guess we still thought of her as our baby girl," Ben said. "She's grown a lot lately, so she probably could reach the latch."

"How long ago did she go missing?" I asked.

"She's been gone since about two this afternoon." Tamara wiped at the tears on her cheeks. She lifted her chin in determination. "What else can we tell you?"

"How is Maddi's health? Does she have any medical conditions that could endanger her life?"

"She's perfectly healthy," Ben said.

"Good. Now, tell me about her personality."

"She's happy and confident," Ben said.

"She loves her animals, stuffed and real," Tamara said. "I mean, she doctors them, changes their clothes, puts on bandages, and even insists on time-outs."

"Maddi adores that cat," Ben said.

"Sasha is a sweet and loving kitten." Tamara's eyes filled with tears. "She sleeps with Maddi, and she'll even sit patiently at tea parties."

"The problem may be that we had Sasha declawed to protect the furniture," Ben said. "We explained to Maddi that Sasha was defenseless without claws. She couldn't climb trees to get to safety. We noticed Sasha wanted to explore outside the yard. We had to bring her back a couple of times."

"If Sasha climbed up and over the fence, we believe Maddi would have followed to save her," Tamara said. "And it's a big world out there."

"Fay is good at her job. We'll do our best to find her." I sounded confident, but I knew many things could prevent a successful search. Yet it was important that everyone stay positive, especially when dealing with rescue dogs. Animals pick up our every emotion through body language, so we must always keep up faith and hope.

"Thank you," Tamara said.

"If it's okay, I'd like to see Maddi's bedroom."

Chapter

Three

Noah, my flanker, and I followed Ben and Tamara upstairs. We stepped into a bright, cheerful pink-and-white bedroom. Toys, dolls, games, and books filled several bookshelves. Stuffed animals were carefully arranged atop a pink ruffled comforter on the bed.

I walked over to a window with sunlight filtering through lace curtains. I looked outside over the terrain Fay and I would be crossing in our search. Prairie grass stretched away to bands of cottonwood and oak trees that grew along creek beds. A little girl could easily get lost out there and be hard to find.

I turned back to Maddi's room. Here, among her things, she came alive to me. I felt her family's loss. Fay and I would do whatever it took to bring this child home.

First, I needed a scent article that would have only Maddi's scent on it. Fay would use Maddi's scent to follow with her nose just like I used my eyes to follow a map. I decided that Maddi's strongest scent would be where she slept.

"Does Maddi sleep in her own bed?" I asked.

"Yes," Tamara said.

"Good."

I opened my scent article bag. I removed a pair of gloves and pulled them on so my own scent wouldn't contaminate the scent article. I took out gauze pads and zip-lock bags. I ripped open two pads and placed one under Maddi's pillow and the other under her covers. I stepped back to wait for the pads to soak up the scent.

After fifteen minutes, I carefully placed the pads in separate baggies and zipped them shut. I wrote Maddi's name on the outside of each bag.

I tucked one in my pocket for Fay and handed Noah the other baggie. He knew to give it to Bowen in case another search team was needed. Normally dogs should be able to work for four to eight hours with brief periods of rest. But if a hard search went over three hours or so, a dog team could get too tired to work well. Another team might be brought in to back them up. I hoped Fay and I would find Maddi right away.

Now that we had the scent articles, we were ready to begin our search. We walked downstairs. Several police officers and other people waited there to help.

"When we begin," I said, "I'd like for all those who may have touched something in Maddi's room to be present. I know all of you have been looking for her. I don't want Fay to follow the wrong person. This way Fay will know who is safe and who is missing in case someone's scent lingers on the scent article."

"Where do you want us to meet you?" Noah asked.

"In the backyard. I'll get Fay and take her there."

"I'll gather everybody," Noah said.

"We'd like to go on the search," Ben said.

I shook my head. "Thanks, but no. You're understandably upset. Out there, we must stay focused on Maddi. Family members might cause problems in the search by putting too much stress on the dog and the handler."

Ben nodded and put his arm around Tamara's shoulders.

"We'll keep you informed of our progress."

"Thanks," Ben said.

"If Maddi is with Sasha, I doubt they went far," I explained. "Cats wander off, but usually they need to nap in between adventures. Dogs roam farther since they don't sleep as often as cats. Hopefully, Maddi and Sasha are safely nearby."

I left Noah with the family and walked back to Fay. We would all rely on her keen sense of smell from here on out.

I considered scent. When I smell a cake baking, I smell the wonderful aroma of an entire cake. Fay smells much more than a cake. She smells each and every ingredient. And she keeps on smelling the ingredients long after I have become accustomed to the cake's scent. Fay follows scent particles that are left behind by someone. As that person moves, the particles fall to the ground and also get caught up on the wind currents. If he puts his hand on a tree as he passes, it's like leaving the dog a note, saying, "I went this way." If he stands still, more and more scent particles fall, which creates a scent pool that can linger for some time after the person has left. This scent pool moves in the shape of a snow cone on the wind currents, spreading outward the farther it gets from the original source. Fay can detect human scent by lost skin cells, dried sweat, exhaled breath, and other sources. She can even catch scent from as far away as a quarter mile or more.

I opened the tailgate of our SUV and set down my scent article kit. Fay jumped from her seat to join me, swishing her tail in eagerness.

I ruffled the thick fur around her neck and then snapped the lead onto her collar. I picked up my heavy search bag, slung it over my shoulders, and felt a strong sense of purpose. My backpack contained Fay's twenty-foot lead and harness, her rescue vest, and her lighted collar. It included my headlamp, flashlight and extra batteries, walkie-talkie, first-aid kit, knife, granola bars, energy mix, compass, GPS (Global Positioning System), and other important items, including a can of Fay's all-important Vienna sausage treats. They are her reward for a job well done.

Fay poked her nose into the pocket of my shirt to check for her reward.

"Yes, your treat is in there." I patted my pocket, feeling three Vienna sausages in a baggie.

They are her favorite treat. She always gets three and knows if I hold out. She also gets another one when she gets back to our SUV after a search. I use this as a reward to avoid a potential dog handler challenge. Some dogs will prolong a training trail because they don't want it to be over because they know they will have to sit in a vehicle and wait. Fay always promptly returns.

"Let's go," I said.

Fay jumped out of the vehicle. She ran to the end of her lead, stopped, and looked back at me, head up, eyes bright. She leaned into her collar, her nose testing the wind. She was all business now.

I added extra water to my backpack and shut the SUV's tailgate. As I called Fay to me, I thought back to our beginning in search and rescue.

Chapter

Four

After the 9/11 attacks, I vowed to do something to help my country. Search and rescue (SAR) proved vital in the aftermath of the attacks. In a magazine, I saw a photo of a dog and a handler on a pallet being lifted by a crane into the rubble to search for survivors. The dog was a golden retriever and wore a bright orange search and rescue vest.

I love helping people, working with dogs, and being outdoors. I decided to train for search and rescue, but I needed a puppy to train.

Not just any dog would do. Breeds matter. First, dogs must be large and strong enough to get through and over obstacles. They must have a strong work ethic and enjoy following their noses. They must be smart and playful. Working and retrieving breeds are especially good at search work. But larger mixed breeds do well too.

One day I met Gary, a rancher. He is a chiropractor by trade, but his passion is for training horses and dogs. He wore a crisp denim shirt and starched jeans. Under an obviously one-of-a-kind hat was blondish-brown hair and intelligent blue eyes. The tobacco-chewing cowboy's thick mustache covered his upper lip.

"I'm looking for a puppy to train as a search and rescue dog," I said. For some time I'd been asking everybody I met if they had an opinion on dog breeds. I figured a man with Gary's experience ought to know animals.

"Do you have a breed in mind?" Gary asked.

"I'm thinking about a Labrador retriever."

"They're smart dogs. I have one of my own. German shepherds and golden retrievers are also good dogs for search and rescue. Bloodhounds too."

I nodded, feeling pleased about my choice.

"Have you thought about a Border collie?"

"Aren't they small? Timid? They're sheepherders, aren't they?"

He chuckled. "Depends on the dog. My Border collies are from a harder, tougher bloodline used to herd and gather cattle and buffalo."

"I didn't realize that."

"Even in our automated world, Border collies are still the best for herding animals on farms and ranches. Their bodies are designed for herding, but they also use 'eye,' an intense, hypnotic stare, to intimidate and control herds. They do the work of three people."

"I'm impressed."

"Good." He leaned forward, warming to his subject. "Let me give you some background on Border collies. They're considered the smartest of all breeds. They've got lots of energy. They're great athletes. And they're highly trainable."

"You can say that for a lot of dogs."

"Yes. But in my opinion, Border collies are better at all of it. They can jump high, run fast, and stop on a dime. And they want to work with people."

"You're trying to change my mind, aren't you?"

He chuckled as he spit a wad of tobacco juice. "How am I doing?"

"Pretty good."

"Well, Border collies are not for everyone. They are truly working dogs and need a job to work off all their extra energy. They can get into trouble and develop bad habits if they don't get the exercise they need."

"Sounds like me," I said with a smile.

He grinned, "Most trainers say if you don't give a Border collie a job, they'll make up one on their own, and you probably won't like it!"

"Border collies come from droving and gathering dog breeds that originated on the Scottish and English border. The Border collie type traces its ancestry to Old Hemp. He was born in September of 1893 and died in May of 1901. Adam Telfer bred Hemp from Roy, a black-and-tan male, and Meg, a solid black female. Old Hemp was known to be a quiet, powerful sheep dog. He left many descendents."

"You must be a breeder."

Gary laughed. "I guess I sound like one." He pulled out his wallet and selected a photograph and held it out. "I worked my way through college training SAR dogs. Now I raise Border collies."

I looked at the photo of two black-and-white dogs sitting beside Gary in a golf cart.

"That's Sam and Lexi. They're both registered Border collies. They're an incredible herding duo. They herd all my critters and then each other." He chuckled again.

"They're gorgeous." I liked Gary. I liked his bright eyes and his ready sense of humor. If he were a dog, I figured he'd be a Border collie. He obviously loved and understood animals. I began to trust him about my puppy. I handed back the photo.

"Fact is, Sam and Lexi are the proud parents of another litter. You might want to come out to the ranch and look at them."

"Oh, I don't know."

"Come take a look. See if one appeals to you. No commitment."

"I might just do that."

"The offspring of Sam and Lexi are active in dog events, trials, and competitions. They win awards all the time."

"I'd like to come see them even if I don't choose a Border collie."

"Border collies make great search and rescue dogs. They're fast and agile. They're highly motivated. They also like to work and are capable of trailing lost livestock over long distances."

"You're making Border collies sound like perfect SAR dogs."

"They are. Come out to the ranch. I've got a puppy in mind that might just work for you."

"I'll do that."

We shook hands, and I went away with his business card.

I debated about seeing his litter of puppies. I wasn't sure about Border collies, even though Gary had made them sound perfect. I had always liked big dogs. On the other hand, you had to be able to carry your dog out if it became sick or injured on the trail. Carrying a forty-pound Border collie would definitely be easier than a hundred-and-ten-pound bloodhound! I chuckled as the picture of me struggling along with a huge bloodhound draped over my shoulders crossed my mind. A Border collie was sounding better and better.

Two weeks later, I dreamed about a black-and-white puppy named Fayva. If I could find this dog, I knew she was the one.

The next day I drove to Gary's ranch near Seminole, Oklahoma. He welcomed me to his home and then hurried me to a big red barn to show off his puppies. When I walked inside, eight black-and-white puppies ran eagerly toward me. They fell over each other as they struggled to get my attention.

One small female sat down at my feet and gazed up at me. She looked smart. I played with her for a moment. She hurried off to search out everything in the barn. She went over hay bales, under the tractor, on top of a pile of fence posts, and around all the puppies.

I noticed a male puppy. He stood back, having nothing to do with anyone. I was drawn to him though I didn't believe he'd make a good SAR dog. The small female puppy took time to lick and nurture the lone male. None of the other puppies approached him.

"I'd like to give that male puppy a loving home."

"Thanks," Gary said. "But I'm keeping him because of his standoffish personality."

"He'll be okay on the ranch?"

"It suits him here. He's got plenty of room to roam." Gary gestured around the barn. "Look. Which puppy do you think would be the best search and rescue dog? But most of all, which one will be your buddy?"

"Will you point out the one you have in mind?"

"It's not for me to say. You choose."

As I glanced around, the busy little female came back by, sat at my feet a moment, and then hurried off to climb, look, and search for something.

I smiled at Gary. "I think she's the one. She picked me out."

The little female scampered over to me and put her front paws on my shins. She looked up as if to say, "I'm your puppy. I'm busy right now. When you get ready to leave, just come get me."

She wasn't the cutest of the puppies. In fact, she was the runt of the litter. She was mostly black. The others were traditionally marked with a wide white stripe up their face and a bright white ruff around their necks. But she was the busy, energetic one. And she liked to search.

"You sure you want that scrawny puppy?" Gary asked, chuckling.

"Yep! She's my puppy."

"That's the one I picked out for you. I think she'll make a good search and rescue dog."

"So do I."

When the small puppy ran back to me, I picked her up and held her close. She happily licked my nose. She gazed at me adoringly with warm brown eyes. I'd nurture and train her until she was the best Border collie she could be—and the very best SAR dog.

I'd found my dream dog. I'd found Fay.

Chapter
Five

As a team, Fay and I had found many lost people. Now we were set to find Maddi. We hurried to the backyard. Maddi's family, police officers, and other search personnel waited for us. They looked tense and anxious.

Bowen and Noah nodded to me in reassurance.

I walked to the middle of the yard. Fay stepped close to me. She stood still as I put on her trailing harness. I custom-made the harness for her because she is so small. Most trailing dogs are larger breeds, so the commercial harnesses are too big and bulky for Fay's delicate frame.

I slipped her orange SAR vest on her. It had RESCUE in big letters and large, white reflective crosses on each side. Finally, I clipped her lead to the D-ring on her harness.

The start of a search was vital, and there was no room for mistakes. I planned to begin where Maddi was last seen. Maddi had played in the backyard a lot. She had probably left from there. It was the best place to start.

"I'd like everyone to please line up side by side so Fay can eliminate your scent from Maddi's scent."

As I watched them get into line, I glanced up at the sky. Daylight was fading. Storm clouds were gathering. And the heat was stifling. I wanted to hurry, but we couldn't. Every step was crucial to the successful outcome of our search.

"Thank you for your cooperation," I said.

"We're glad to do everything we can to help," Ben replied, clutching Tamara's hand.

I led Fay by them so she could get a good sniff of each person. By this she knew that these people were not lost. Now we'd search for the one who was missing.

"Everyone except Noah please step outside the fence."

As a fireman, Noah was trained in SAR work. He would be flanking for us. He'd make sure we were okay, keep in touch with the I.C., and watch the weather. He'd also help us search and keep up with our location so we didn't get lost.

After everyone else stood outside the fence, I pulled out the scent article. I opened the baggie, taking care not to touch the scent pad. I held out the bag.

"Mark it!"

Fay dipped her nose to the baggie and sniffed. She looked up into my eyes to tell me she'd got it.

We had performed this routine many times in training and real searches. I used the same routine every time so she knew what was coming.

I leaned down close to her face. "Are you ready to work?"

She bunched her strong muscles as she went into a full-body crouch just inches off the ground.

In this position, she looked like a typical Border collie focusing on the job ahead. I knew she was ready to get to work.

"Go find!"

Fay sprang into action. She weaved all around the yard, searching for Maddi. She circled around the bushes. She circled around the playhouse. She circled around the swing set. She leaped up onto the porch. She checked the backdoor. She nosed around the trashcans. She ran round the inside of the fence.

As I watched Fay work, I stood still in the middle of the yard as I played out my long lead. I gave Fay plenty of room and lead length. I didn't want to influence or distract her in any way. She would determine Maddi's direction of travel by scent.

Finally Fay circled to the closed back gate. She stopped. She put her nose to the bottom where it met the ground. She sniffed hard. She nudged the gate with her nose. She glanced back at me.

Fay's message came loud and clear. Maddi had gone out the gate. We could follow her and hopefully bring her safely home.

"Maddi went out the back gate," I called over my shoulder to the group of people anxiously waiting.

I turned toward Ben and Tamara. "Maddi went out the back gate."

Tamara's eyes filled with tears.

"She followed Sasha like we thought?" Ben asked.

"We won't know for sure till we find her. But I think so."

"And now?" Tamara asked.

"We follow Fay."

"Hurry," Tamara said.

"Bring our little girl home," Ben said.

I nodded. "Have faith in Fay."

Chapter

Six

Noah pushed open the back gate.

Fay didn't hesitate. The waiting was over. It was time to get to work. With her nose low to the ground, she started her trail.

I lined up behind her, giving her the full length of the lead so she had plenty of room to work. Fortunately, her twenty-foot lead is rubber coated, so it won't catch on cactus or briars. She likes her lead to stay in the middle of her back. If it slides over, she gets distracted by it.

Most trailing dogs pull hard on the lead. Fay doesn't. I trained her not to pull on the lead when I first taught her obedience, before I knew much about SAR work. Later in training her to trail, I was challenged because she was handler-oriented. If I pulled too hard or stepped on the lead, she would stop and look at me as if to say, "You don't want me to do that?" Now that we are both more experienced and confident, she will sometimes lightly tug me in the direction we need to go. Most of the time I rely heavily on the use of body language instead of the lead to read her.

Noah and I followed Fay's trail, plowing through knee-high prairie grass made up of Johnson grass, Queen Anne's Lace, and other wildflowers. We kept watch for Maddi's footprints or other signs, such as broken stems, that she had passed this way. But we found nothing to help our search.

Fay trotted in her standard trailing mode, her tail straight out and stiff. She kept her body and head in a straight line. Her ears flicked to the side but stayed pricked up. Her nose might be down or straight out. Sometimes she wagged her tail. I wasn't surprised. She loved children, and she was following a little girl.

Fay's body language told me that we were on the right trail. We'd spent hours learning to understand each other. The longer we worked together, the stronger our team. My job was to follow Fay. I supported her. I refocused her if she became distracted. I cast her farther out if she got hung up in a scent pool or lost the trail. On occasion, she might even experience a bad day. I had to remain positive no matter the situation. My feelings travel right down the lead to Fay, so I keep negative thoughts out of my mind.

Fay pushed through grass taller than her head. She wove back and forth under bushes and through brambles. I noticed the trail fit the pattern of a six-year-old looking for her beloved cat. It had to be just a matter of time before we found Maddi.

Noah fanned out to the side. He checked ditches and thick clumps of grass where a child could hide. He called out to Maddi when Fay showed a strong interest in an area.

Occasionally, Fay bounced up out of the tall grass to test the air for scent. She'd drop down and be gone again.

Soon the heat left me drenched with sweat. Flies and mosquitoes buzzed my face. I watched out for snakes such as poisonous rattlers and copperheads, but I couldn't see much in the tall, thick grass. The air was stifling, humid with rain in the area. My backpack felt like it weighed a ton.

We struggled forward, leaving the house and roads behind. We cast long shadows before us as the sun lowered in the west.

Finally, we tramped out of the thick grass into a mowed hay field. Now the going would be faster and easier for us all.

Ahead, Fay quickly zigzagged along the trail. She often lifted her head to test the wind for scent.

We were all hot and tired. I decided we needed a break and to regroup. I called to Fay to wait, motioned to Noah, and he walked over.

"I'd hoped to find Maddi by now." I set down my backpack.

"I wish we had," he agreed.

"I can see rain in the distance."

"It's coming our way."

I pulled two bottles of water out of my bag. I handed one to Noah. We both eagerly drank until we felt better.

Up to this point, Fay had been on-lead, following close to Maddi's trail. If I took her off-lead, she could range far ahead at her own pace, cover more ground, pick up fresh scent on the air, and perhaps reach Maddi before the storm hit. I couldn't hope to walk that fast.

"We're moving too slow," I said. "I'm worried about the storm."

"I'll call base for a weather update," Noah said.

"I'll check the topo map."

I glanced at Fay. She sat right where she had stopped, facing where Maddi had gone. She scratched her ear with a hind foot.

While Noah called, I pulled out my topographical map. We always carried a map of the search and rescue area. It showed dirt, gravel, and paved roads, lakes, rivers, and creeks, and the lay of the land, like hills and mountains. Right now I looked for valleys or dry creek beds that could fill with runoff water before the rain even reached us. My concern increased when I saw that several dry creek beds crisscrossed in front of us. Lost people naturally headed downhill because it was easier. They might also look for shelter in a dry creek bed. It was a dangerous area when rainwater from a storm rushed down the creeks.

I feared for Maddi and Sasha.

"Storm won't miss us," Noah said as he hung up with the I.C.

"We've got dry creek beds ahead." I folded the map and put it in my pocket.

"Not dry for long."

"I know," I said with a sigh. "Faith in Fay."

"What did you say?" he asked, puzzled.

"Faith in Fay. That's my motto. It's to remind me to trust my dog when the odds are stacked against us."

Fay stood up at the mention of her name and leaned into the leash.

As I stood at the edge of the mowed pasture, I felt a strong wind on my face. The storm was getting closer. We had to hurry. I walked to Fay and bent over, squeezing the drinking tube on my backpack, squirting out water.

Fay lapped up the water till she drank her fill. She panted, pink tongue hanging out to keep her cool in the heat. She looked up at me and then looked ahead.

I knew what she meant. She wanted to get back to work. I hesitated. We weren't near roads or vehicles, so Fay was safe from that danger. Rain and night were nearly upon us. I unsnapped the lead from Fay's harness.

"Get to work!" I said.

She darted off and ranged far ahead.

Noah and I followed. He called out for Maddi while I kept focused on Fay. We also checked the ground for Maddi's flower shoe prints. But we found no sign of her.

Up ahead, Fay stopped and stood completely still. She focused on the ground, her head down.

I'd never seen her do that before. A chill of foreboding ran up my spine.

What was wrong with Fay?

Chapter

Seven

"Noah!" I called. "Fay needs us."

"Trouble?"

"I don't know. We need to find out."

We jogged across the mowed field. Insects flew up and away as we sent clouds of dust into the air. We stopped beside Fay.

She ignored everything around her, eyes intently downcast.

I knelt beside her, hoping she hadn't been bitten by a snake. I remembered to push that negative thought from my mind so I wouldn't influence her. I realized she couldn't move.

"Fay, what's going on?" I asked, keeping my voice soft and even.

She jerked up her head. A sticker was lodged between her teeth. She spit it out and bent her head to her upturned foot to pull out another one.

"Let me see."

As I gently nudged Fay's head aside, I grasped her paw and gasped. Sharp stickers stuck to the bottom of her paw. She'd run through a sand burr patch made up of thick clumps of stickers about the size of a pea and the color of dry grass with quarter-inch-long spikes on all sides. She had to be in pain. She couldn't take a step without driving the stickers deeper.

I gently released Fay's paw, squatted, picked her up, and turned her upside down across my thighs. All four of her paws were covered in stickers. She didn't like being in that vulnerable position, particularly when there was work to be done. But she trusted me to take care of her.

"Hold still, girl. Let me pull out the burrs."

Fay exhaled in response but remained patient, her nose testing the wind as she caught some scent.

I felt the urgency of the moment as we took time away from the search. The storm was coming, clouds gathering, wind picking up.

As I pulled out the barbed stickers, my fingers got pricked and sore. I imagined how much Fay's paws must be hurting her. Yet she didn't whine or complain. She gave a little jerk now and again to remind me that she needed to get back to her important work.

I removed the last of the stickers. To make sure I hadn't missed a burr, I checked between the toes of her paws. I didn't see any more so I flipped her over and held her in my arms as I walked a short distance away from the sand burr patch. I checked the soles of my boots to make sure

I hadn't picked up stickers. No burrs. I looked around. I stood on safe ground.

Fay gave me a quick thank-you lick and jerked a little to get free. I understood she wanted to get back to work. She was right. We needed to get going. A little girl depended on us. I set Fay down.

She shook her fur as if to get rid of any last stickers and then lifted her nose, testing the wind. She glanced back, waiting.

Fortunately, she was okay. She didn't seem to notice any discomfort from the stickers. But I still hurt. I rubbed my stinging fingers against my jeans to relieve the pain.

"You both okay?" Noah asked.

"Yes. Let's just stay out of any more sand burr patches."

"I'll keep an eye out for them."

"Okay, Fay," I said. "Let's go. Let's go."

Fay lifted her nose and caught scent on the wind. She set off again, weaving back and forth. Then her body language suddenly switched to trailing mode, and she lined out on a trail.

"How do you know if Fay is on the right track?" Noah asked. "If she's not, we're losing valuable time."

"Remember, have faith in Fay."

As I turned to look at him, I saw something on the ground slightly ahead of us. I hurried over and leaned down for a closer look.

I thrust a fist triumphantly into the air. "Noah, here!"

We looked at a small shoe's tread imprinted in the soft dirt. A cat's paw print nestled beside it.

"Maddi and Sasha came this way."

"Yes!" he exclaimed.

We leaned down to closely examine the print. The faint, partial imprint of a flower marked the shoe's tread. We had solid evidence that we were on the right track.

"Faith in Fay," Noah said.

I nodded, feeling relief as I watched Fay's tail wave from the trail ahead.

Now we had concrete proof that Maddi hadn't been picked up by a stranger and taken away. I felt a renewed sense of energy and urgency to find her as the storm drew nearer and day turned to night.

Noah keyed the radio. "We've found a footprint. Maddi is definitely in the area. Stand by for the coordinates."

While Noah gave our exact location to the I.C., I checked on Fay. I didn't want her to get too far ahead while we marked the print locations.

"Fay, wait!"

She stopped. She didn't turn around or look back. She kept her nose pointed in the direction of the trail.

I knew she wanted to keep going, but we had to secure the prints first.

Noah keyed off the radio and clipped it back on his belt. He pulled a roll of bright pink flagging tape out of his pocket, tore off two strips, and tied the strips to two sticks. He stuck a stick into the ground near each print.

Now we could be sure that searchers coming behind us wouldn't accidentally step on the prints and destroy the evidence. If the rain came, we couldn't stop it from washing away the prints, but at least we'd followed procedure and flagged them.

"Ready?" I asked.

"Yes." Noah stuffed the flagging tape in his pocket.

"Get to work," I called to Fay in a happy voice.

She surged forward and picked up speed.

I could tell she was happy to be free of the slower-moving people. I watched as her head snapped up and down. She ran a zigzag pattern. It meant she'd found a fresher, stronger scent in the air. She was no longer trailing on the ground. Off-lead, she was airscenting. Hopefully we were fairly close to Maddi.

The wind came to us from the direction Maddi seemed to have gone. That meant Maddi's scent was coming toward Fay, spreading outward from the little girl. Fay ran within the cone-shaped scent to the edge of the field, and then she turned back.

When Fay ran up to me, I knelt down to her level and ruffled the fur around her neck. She was checking in before she entered the woods.

"Good, girl," I said. "Let's go, let's go!"

Fay spun around and took off. She reached the edge of the field and disappeared into the thick stand of trees.

Chapter
Eight

Noah and I jogged across the empty field. Two legs were definitely slower than four. I watched the place where Fay disappeared into the woods to make sure we didn't take a wrong turn and lose time.

I glanced up at the sky. Dark clouds scudded closer. I felt apprehension from head to toe.

"We'd better find Maddi quick," Noah said. "That storm isn't waiting for us."

"It looks bad."

"Let's hurry."

We pushed harder.

My heart pounded in my chest. I struggled to get more air in my lungs. My backpack felt like I was hauling bricks, but I pushed on. Nothing mattered except finding Maddi.

Noah and I made it to the woods and stopped, gasping for breath. We drank water, sloshing it over our faces to cool down.

While Noah called to Maddi, I focused on keeping Fay in sight.

We faced a change of weather and terrain. Trees blocked the wind, so the air was hot and still. Thick tree trunks and undergrowth created a natural barrier that made the going harder. Birds sang in the treetops, but when we walked forward, they grew silent.

I caught glimpses of Fay through the trees as we moved in her general direction. She swung back and forth as she worked her way down the scent cone toward Maddi. She ran in one direction, and then turned back when she ran out of scent at the edge.

We caught up to Fay because we walked in a straight line while she weaved back and forth.

When I got a good look at her, she was panting heavily. I felt concerned that she'd gotten overheated. She had to cool down or she'd get sick.

"Fay, wait!" I commanded.

She stopped, but kept looking in the direction she'd been headed.

I knelt beside her, and she bunched her muscles to start.

"Wait," I said again quietly, "you're okay." She relaxed, the familiar phrase and tone of voice keeping her from starting on the trail again.

I squeezed the drinking tube on my backpack, squirting out water. By doing this I sent her the message to finish drinking water and catch her breath.

Fay lapped up the water, relaxed, and flopped on the ground, pink tongue hanging out as she panted to get cool.

People can cool quickly by sweating from pores all over their bodies, but dogs only cool down through their mouths and paw pads. They can easily overheat and then not be able to get cool very fast.

Still concerned about Fay, I poured water over her belly to help her cool down as quickly as possible. She squeezed her eyes shut in pleasure.

"How is she?" Noah asked.

"She's fine. She's a tough little cookie."

"Good," he said. "I hate to mention it, but it'll be dark soon, harder to see."

The sky had definitely darkened. I couldn't tell if it was dusk or the storm clouds reaching us. Either way, we needed to move as soon as Fay recovered her energy.

"Faith in Fay," I said.

"I trust her," Noah said. "But night makes a difference for us."

"This'll help." I pulled Fay's lighted collar from my backpack. I snapped it around her neck and turned it on. The collar emitted a bluish bright glow. Now I could spot her at a distance. Fortunately, the light wasn't so bright that it hurt her eyes and caused her to lose her night vision. She could see fine wearing it.

"Perfect," Noah said. "We just need to stay close enough to her to see the collar."

"Good girl." I ruffled Fay's thick, dark fur as I stood up. Fay leaped up.

Thunder rumbled in the distance.

Fay dipped her head and flattened her ears.

"You're okay." I hooked an arm under her belly and pulled her backward between my legs. I picked up her front end and gave her smooth belly a pat while I hugged her. She gave me a dog grin as I released her.

"What's wrong?" Noah asked.

"Fay hates thunderstorms. But she won't let it distract her from her job."

"She's a real professional."

"Fay, get to work!"

Fay shook her body as if to shake away the worry of thunder. She bolted back to following the scent cone.

Noah keyed his radio and called in our position.

We set out again. I followed Fay. Noah worked the trail to the side, calling out to Maddi.

In the woods, the heat felt worse than in the fields. Insects buzzed my head. I shooed them away. They came back. Thunder rumbled closer. Humidity rose.

I came to a ditch about a foot wide and two feet deep. As I stepped over it, I looked down. Water trickled through the dusty ditch, picking up speed and volume as it came. My worst fears were confirmed. Rain from the distant storm was already rolling down to the low areas and dry creek beds.

"Noah!" I pointed toward the ditch. "Water! We're running out of time."

He rushed over. "Maddi won't understand how a gully washer might knock her off her feet. Even though it's dry here, she could be in a low area that will quickly fill with water."

"Let's hurry."

We jogged forward.

I watched Fay's behavior. She appeared more animated. She worked quickly, her ears pricked, her tail occasionally wagging as she hit fresh scent, a good indication the scent was getting stronger. Surely we were close to Maddi.

Fay stayed mostly out of sight as she ran through the woods. I caught glimpses of her here and there. I didn't need any more than that to stay on her trail.

As I topped a low rise, I felt cool, wet wind hit my face. Leaves rattled as rain fell in fat, heavy drops that soon turned to sheets of water. I lost sight of Fay and slowed to a walk. I couldn't take a chance on going the wrong direction.

Noah caught up to me. We walked toward a small, sheltered place where we might still find Fay's paw prints.

As we stepped into the area, a wall of rain swept in so hard that it knocked me back against Noah. We both got soaked to the skin. We searched for Fay's prints, but the rain had destroyed any sign of her that might have been in the dirt.

We stopped. We didn't know which direction to go. Without Fay to lead us, rain, thunder, and wind made going forward impossible. We huddled down close to the ground with our backs to the stinging wind.

"I'm worried." I leaned toward Noah. "Maddi may be in a low area. Fay is afraid of loud storms. Maddi might get washed away."

Noah reminded me: "Have faith in Fay."

"You're right," I agreed. "Fay won't let us down."

She had earned my trust time and again. She would alert me to where she was or if she made the find. I just had to wait for her to come to me. I had to believe that she was doing what she had been trained to do. We hadn't been called by chance to save Maddi. We had worked hard to become a rescue team.

Chapter

Nine

When I brought Fay home from Gary's ranch, she was an eager puppy. We started obedience training, and she learned quickly and easily. First, she mastered simple commands such as stay, sit, down. Soon after that, we started search training. Fay eagerly responded to all the training as if she knew the importance of our work.

I didn't know enough to get the best results from her. I needed training as a handler. I read books on training a search dog and combed the web for information.

Fortunately, a friend of mine had trained and shown dogs in American Kennel Club tracking. Although AKC tracking is competition only and not search work, we started her on short, straight trails.

Fay loved it all. She approached training with great enthusiasm. Soon she was running trails. Later, I found out I hadn't used the normal method for training search dogs. Search dogs have to get to the victim the quickest way possible, on the strongest scent. They are not trained to follow a trail footprint to footprint. Fortunately, Fay was smart enough to overcome my inexperience.

I got her pretty far along with books, but I needed professional help. Fay was growing up and needed immediate training. I found a seminar in southern Louisiana and signed up for it.

It was a long drive. We didn't get there until after dark. The seminar was being held in a national park on the shores of Lake Pontchartrain. After the long drive, I thought Fay might like a swim. We stopped. I threw sticks into the lake for her to fetch. We had great fun.

At orientation the next morning, the trainer warned us not to let our dogs near the water. Lake Pontchartrain's large alligator population might attack. I was horrified. I might have lost Fay. I vowed to be more careful in the future.

I had enrolled us in an airscent class because the experts advised that Fay would be better at it than at trailing. Airscent is done with the dog off-lead. The dog ranges over a wider area than on-lead, searching for whatever human scent might be in that area. As a puppy, Fay wouldn't range very far, probably due to her natural Border collie herding instincts.

We learned a lot at that seminar, but I still felt like I needed a better understanding of how to advance our search and rescue work. I signed up for a seminar in Mississippi. We went a day early so we could relax before classes.

Fay and I sat on a picnic table, getting used to the area. People walked by us following a dog on a trail. Their instructor said, "What is the dog doing? What is the dog telling you?"

When I heard him ask those two questions, I knew what I was missing as a handler. I didn't know how to read my dog.

The instructor saw me and asked me to come along. I did. He immediately hooked me with his knowledge. I was so impressed with his technique that later I requested to be transferred to his class.

In our first class, he looked at me and asked, "What do you want to get out of your seminar experience?"

"I want to be a part of the solution and not part of the problem."

"Good," he said. "What else?"

"If I can't be a good handler, or if Fay isn't a good search dog prospect, I want to know by the end of the seminar."

"You got it," he said.

We went on to learn a lot from him and the other handlers and dogs. Fay enjoyed the classes and attention.

After the seminar, the instructor took me aside. "Don't you dare quit search and rescue. And don't you dare quit this dog," he said.

"Thank you." I grinned, bubbling over with happiness. I knew he meant that he thought Fay and I were good enough to continue. "I'll never quit Fay. And we'll never quit search and rescue."

"That's what I wanted to hear."

He gave me the names of people to help us when we got back home. I contacted them and we became good friends. They helped train Fay and me, even though they mostly worked with bloodhounds. They honed our skills with tough trails and hard problems, never letting us fail in training. As our knowledge and confidence grew under their friendship and guidance, Fay and I bonded as a team. One year later, we passed our Mission Ready Test. We were a K-9 Search and Rescue Team.

Fay was the only trailing Border collie in our group. She also works off-lead as an airscent dog. She does double duty in search and rescue.

At that time, I still wanted to be involved in disaster work. I wanted a disaster dog that searched through rubble for buried survivors caused by earthquakes, bombings, mudslides, hurricanes, and other disasters. I learned that FEMA controls it all and requires a dog to deliver a fifteen second continuous bark alert when they find a victim.

Fay's bloodline had been bred not to bark to keep from disrupting the herd, so barking was not natural to her, and SAR dogs respond best under stress when trained to their natural strengths.

Several people suggested that I get another dog. I quickly decided against it. If FEMA wasn't for Fay, then I wasn't for disaster work.

We stayed in search and rescue where Fay was best suited to help others. As the years passed, our bond deepened into a level of understanding that only comes with constant close contact. We were a unit. We worked as one.

Chapter

Ten

Rain pelted down hard on us as the storm raged overhead. I strained to catch a glimpse of Fay's lighted collar in the darkness. Nothing. She'd been gone for some time now. Fay always checked back to make sure I was coming when she ranged far ahead. Maybe she was checking on me, but I couldn't see her in the rain.

I didn't take out my headlamp or a flashlight because they ruin my night vision. I can see farther with night vision than with a light that only reveals small areas at a time. I only use lamps or lights as a last resort. So far, I could see well enough without extra light.

As I waited, I thought about Fay and her keen sense of smell. One time I tested her ability to trail in the rain. A practice trail was laid down the middle of a creek. The trail-layer climbed out on the opposite bank a hundred yards downstream and continued the trail through the woods. I planned to come back the following afternoon and run the trail with her. That night, a big storm blew in and rained heavily in the area. I went to the creek the next day, but it was flooded. The water was three feet deep instead of the usual six inches or so. Two days later we came back. The water was down to its usual flow. I hooked Fay up and decided to see what would happen. She trailed right down the creek bed and climbed out exactly where the trail-layer had exited.

I knew she could follow Maddi's scent in the rain because of that experience, but I'd waited long enough. I pulled out my shepherd's whistle that hung on a lanyard around my neck to call her back. It doesn't really look like a whistle. It's a small, flat piece of aluminum shaped like a half moon with a hole in the back and hollow in the middle. The whole whistle fits between my teeth. I push my tongue against the back of it. Shepherds use this type of whistle to signal commands to their dogs while gathering sheep and bringing them to the pen. Dogs can hear the sound a long distance away.

I put the whistle between my teeth and blew a long, shrill, "Wee-ooo-wheet!"

"Hope that brings Fay," Noah said.

"It will."

I waited, straining to see through the rain.

Fay appeared out of the darkness. She raced up the trail, muddy water flying around her. She slammed to a stop at my feet and sat down.

"She's found Maddi!" I cried.

I knew she had found Maddi because she was trained to assume a "sit" position in front of me to indicate that she had found her lost person. Relief and happiness filled me.

"Let's go get Maddi." Noah stood up.

"Show me!" I commanded.

Fay wheeled around and disappeared into the rain and darkness.

I knew she could hardly wait for us to get to the lost person. She has very strong victim loyalty. Not all dogs have this trait. She is especially loyal to children and hates to leave them once she has found them. Many dogs are trained for a bark alert. They stay with the lost person and bark until the handler arrives. Fay will bark only at intruders. She would never bark near children since she would not want to startle or frighten them.

Noah and I splashed through muddy water after Fay. Reaching the spot where she turned off the trail, we followed her paw prints in the mud, weaving here and there around bushes. We ducked under limbs to stay behind her, but before we knew it the rain had washed away her prints.

We stopped. We'd lost Fay again.

Fay didn't check back with me. I knew she must have found Maddi. She'd presented a "sit" to me. There was no other reason she would have left me without checking back. At least, I hoped there was no other reason. A knot of fear tightened my stomach as I desperately searched for Fay's tracks.

I turned to Noah. "Something's wrong!"

Chapter
Eleven

"Are you sure?" Noah asked, peering through the heavy rain.

"Fay's not acting normal. She always returns to make sure I'm following her." I pushed through thick shrubs and found a faint mark of Fay's trail. "Here!"

Noah joined me to look at Fay's trail, but it was already gone. I glanced around, not knowing which direction to go. Rain hid almost everything.

"Maybe Fay ran into stickers again and can't walk," Noah said. "She might be hung up in vines or something."

"I know. I'm worrying about Maddi too."

"If they're in a low area, this rain will fill up dry creek beds fast."

"Don't even think it. Let's keep going."

We plunged on through the forest, hoping we were going in the right direction. We looked for Fay's lighted collar, but we could see little in the rain.

As we struggled forward, an eerie sound carried above the wind and rain and then faded away.

Noah stopped. "What was that?"

I stopped too.

We held our breath as we listened, desperate for any sound or sign of our lost ones.

A longer, stronger howl rode the wind and swirled through the forest.

"Sounds like a coyote or a wolf," Noah said. "That animal is close. If it's rabid, we're all in trouble."

I smiled even as I felt the hair on the back of my neck stand up in a primal response to the sound. "That's Fay! She's with Maddi."

"You sure?"

"Yes! Come on. We can follow her howls."

I led Noah as we tore through thick brush, heedless of thorns, mud, and tree limbs. We slipped and slid through the falling rain. Thunder rumbled around us. Wind tore at our clothes. Yet we kept going, following Fay's howls.

"Why doesn't Fay bark like other SAR dogs?" Noah yelled through the noise of the rain and the slap of the thick brush against his body.

"She's not trained to bark alert, but she learned to howl from coyotes on the ranch where she was born." I struggled over a fallen tree. "Fay has never done this before. She must be howling to help us find her. And Maddi."

I thought about how Fay loves to howl. She learned to harmonize with coyotes on the ranch. She takes great pleasure in talking in her own language. She has a beautiful voice too. She throws up her head and makes wonderful, eerie sounds. She taught me to howl with her. We frequently howl together, even if it does make the neighbors wonder about us.

As Noah and I struggled through the woods, we followed Fay's howls. We changed course several times. We ran as fast as we could through the underbrush. Lightning flashed in the sky, helping to light our way.

Finally the storm moved slowly across us. The rain slackened and the sky brightened. We could see better. We crashed out of thick brush and onto an old dirt road that hadn't been used in ages. The road ran over a culvert on a normally dry creek bed.

Fay's howls grew louder and more intense.

We ran down the road, looking everywhere for Fay and Maddi. They had to be nearby. We peered through the steady sprinkle of rain.

"There!" I pointed toward the bright blue glow of Fay's collar.

"Faith in Fay!" Noah hollered, excited and pleased.

As we jogged forward, we heard the sound of rushing water. The blue glow of Fay's collar disappeared. We exchanged worried looks.

We reached the creek bank and looked down. In the gloom, we saw an occasional small red flash along with the blue glow of Fay's collar.

The red flashes had to be Maddi's shoes.

In the glow of Fay's collar, we watched her slowly and carefully climbing the bank, just ahead of the wild water that was quickly filling the creek. A wet, bedraggled little girl gripped the fur on Fay's back with one hand and clutched a wet, limp cat in the other. With each step she took, her shoes flashed red. She sobbed quietly.

Tears of happiness mingled with the rain on my face. I realized that after Fay made sure we saw her collar, she went back down to help Maddi up the slippery slope.

I rushed up to them and fell to my knees in the mud. I pulled Maddi and Sasha into my arms and hugged them hard to reassure them, as well as myself, that all was well.

Fay nosed into our group, licking Maddi and Sasha, and then jumped back. She cavorted around us with her tail wagging in happiness. She performed a play bow, and then raced around us in circles, slinging mud in all directions.

As if on cue, the rain slackened to a few large drops, and soon only splatters of water rolled off the thick leaves of the trees. The storm was over, and a child was found.

Noah knelt beside us. He pulled out his radio. "Dog team to base, come in." He grinned. "We've got Maddi and Sasha."

I grinned back at him in happiness.

"All's well." He spoke into the radio. "Thanks to one smart, brave dog named Fay."

Chapter
Twelve

Noah held out his radio. We all heard the whoops and cheers of happiness from the I.C. and Maddi's parents.

I felt like cheering too. Instead, I remained calm and quiet for the child in my arms as the weather quickly improved, the sky lightening, the air cooling. I could smell the wet earth all round us.

"Maddi, you're okay now," I said. "You're safe. We'll take care of you. Fay found you and led us to you."

I felt her nod her head against my shoulder even as her little body shivered with wet and cold. She smelled like wet cat.

"I'm going to get you warm now. Okay?"

She nodded again.

"Your mommy and daddy are waiting for you. We'll take you to them soon."

I pulled off my backpack and set it beside us where I could reach it easily. Noah spread out the plastic sheet I handed him, and I sat down cross-legged on it with Maddi in my lap. She cuddled Sasha close.

We needed my rescue supplies. I could tell Maddi was more scared than anything else, but she needed immediate attention too. I unzipped the main compartment of my rescue bag and rummaged for the things I needed to make Maddi comfortable before we began the long hike home.

Fay didn't wait for supplies. She licked Maddi's face, arms, hands, and legs. She treated the little girl as if she were one of her own puppies. This was Fay's way of reassuring Maddi that she was safe and loved. She wasn't fond of cats, but she gave Sasha a lick every so often so she wouldn't feel left out.

Maddi giggled. "That tickles."

I smiled in relief. Maddi's giggle told me that she had come through her ordeal with flying colors. "Fay is letting you know how much she likes you."

Now I needed to finish the job Fay started. Even though Maddi was wet, I could get her warm. I pulled a black plastic trash bag out of my backpack. Turning the bag upside down, I used my knife to cut a hole large enough for Maddi's face about six inches from the corner along the side. I cut two more holes for her arms.

I took Sasha out of Maddi's arms and held up the wet, spiky-furred kitten.

Noah tucked Sasha into the crook of his arm as he talked on the radio, making final rescue plans with Bowen, our Incident Commander.

I pulled the trash bag over Maddi's head, making sure her face popped through the hole. I pulled her arms through the other two holes. Now she wore a poncho that would retain her body heat. Plastic bags are very useful, but I always make sure of proper ventilation and supervision when I use them with children.

Noah handed Sasha back to me and then left to scout the area.

I dried Sasha with a hand towel from my backpack and then wrapped her up in it to keep her warm.

Maddi and I sat down together. I pulled Maddi into my lap for warmth and reassurance and tucked Sasha into her arms. When they were comfortable, I pulled a bottle of water from my backpack, unscrewed the top, and held it out.

Maddi set Sasha on her lap, took the bottle, and noisily gulped water.

I felt a nudge on the pocket of my shirt.

Fay sat and watched me expectantly.

I had nearly forgotten her reward for a job well done. I reached into my pocket and brought out the baggie containing three Vienna sausages.

Fay wagged her tail in approval.

I took out one sausage and gave it to Fay. "You are a very good girl. I'm proud of you for finding Maddi. You are such a smart dog. Thank you."

I handed Maddi the second sausage so she could reward Fay.

She looked at the sausage, looked at Fay, and then took a big bite. She giggled as she handed what was left of the sausage to Fay.

Fay swallowed the bite in one big gulp.

I gave the third sausage to Sasha. She slipped out of her towel, daintily ate her food, and then cleaned her face and damp fur with a long, pink tongue.

With Fay's reward taken care of, I rummaged through my backpack for more food. I pulled out an extra can of Vienna sausages, three granola bars, and more water.

Noah knelt beside us. He held out a wet, purple bear.

"Snuggles!" Maddi grabbed the bear and held it close. "Thank you! I had to let him go when Fay came to get us."

"You did right," Noah said.

As if a dam had burst, Maddi kept talking. "I got in that place where it was dry, but the rain kept coming down. It got my feet wet, then my knees. Fay came. I was glad. But she left. I had to hold on to Sasha." Maddi lowered her voice. "She was scared. I wasn't. Well, maybe a little."

"You are a brave girl," I said.

"Fay came back," Maddi continued her story. "I worried that she'd go again. I had to drop Snuggles when I grabbed hold of Fay's fur so she wouldn't leave us. I cried when Snuggles floated away."

"You did right," Noah said.

"I held on to Fay, and she pulled us right out of that pipe. I kept slipping in the mud. And then you came." Maddi beamed at everyone.

"And then we came," Noah repeated Maddi's words, a catch in his voice.

"It's why we rescue, isn't it?" I swallowed hard against my own rising emotion.

"Every life saved is a life lived," he said.

"Let's have a tea party!" Maddi looked at Noah and patted the muddy ground beside her.

"Might as well while we wait." Noah sat down. "Bowen is sending an ATV to pick us up. We're lucky they figured out where this old road goes. We won't have to go back the hard way."

"That's good news," I said.

Maddi handed around bottled water, Vienna sausages, and granola bars.

I didn't know when food had tasted so good. We sang a few campfire songs. Fay joined us with some fine howling. And the sky brightened when a huge moon beamed through the scattering clouds.

Fay stood up, looked toward the road, and then woofed a low bark.

Chapter
Thirteen

"What's going on with Fay?" Noah asked.

"Party's over." I stood up. "She hears the four-wheeler."

"I don't hear it," Noah said.

"Me neither," Maddi agreed.

"Fay hears a lot better than we do," I said.

"She does a lot of things better than we do." Noah stood up. "Let's pack up our trash and get ready to go."

I quickly stuffed everything into my backpack and hefted it onto my shoulders.

When our little bedraggled group walked up the dirt road, we could hear the four-wheeler too.

"That's some smart dog," Noah said.

Maddi hugged Fay and then giggled as Fay licked her face.

An ATV with bright headlights came round the bend and made a quick stop, sending mud flying. Bowen stepped down.

"Now I know what Fay was woofing about when she heard the four-wheeler," I said as I walked over to him.

"What?" Bowen asked.

"She knew it was you long before she ever saw you."

Fay tossed her head up and flicked her ears back to the side so far the tips touched. She swept her tail from side to side as far as it would go as she raced over to Bowen.

"Good girl." Bowen knelt down and rubbed behind her ears.

Fay licked his face, tongue hanging out in happiness.

I chuckled. "Fay is such a flirt with you."

Bowen laughed too. "She knows I've got Vienna sausages."

Fay wagged her tail, threw back her head, and howled.

"I feel the same way," Noah said. "Let's get back and get some chow."

We all loaded onto the four-wheeler. Maddi held Sasha and sat on the seat behind Bowen. I sat on one side of Maddi on the rack and Noah sat on the other side of her. Fay loved to go four-wheeling, so she rode on the front so she wouldn't miss any of the action or the great smells as the wind blew across her face and made her long, silky hair flutter.

Maddi laughed with delight as Bowen drove us away.

A trip that had taken hours in the scorching sun and blinding rain took only moments in reverse. Bowen veered off the old dirt road and brought us right up to the backyard. He stopped behind Maddi's home.

As we stepped off the four-wheeler, Ben and Tamara came running out the back gate. They lifted Maddi up into a big bear hug. She laughed and hugged them back.

We all walked into the lighted backyard where more people hurried out to greet us. Soon everyone was hugging and crying and laughing together. Fay frolicked around us, high-spirited and happy. Job well done.

Ben and Tamara walked over. He held Maddi. She held Sasha.

"We can't thank you enough," Ben said.

"Fay is Maddi's rescuer," Tamara added.

"She just did her job," I said.

Fay bounded over.

Maddi got down and stroked Fay's head. "You're the best dog in the whole world."

Ben bent down on one knee and took Fay's head in his hands. He gazed into her warm brown eyes. "Thank you for bringing my girl back. You're a good dog!"

Fay licked his hand in understanding.

"She says you're welcome," I said.

When Ben stood up, his eyes were bright with tears. He held out his hand.

I shook it.

"If there's ever anything I can do for you or Fay, let me know," he said.

"There is something you can do. Please volunteer. Search and rescue always needs help. There are many different types of jobs available."

Maddi threw her arms around Fay's neck. "I want a search dog just like Fay. I'll help find little lost kids. Or can I have a search cat?" she asked seriously.

"I've never heard of one," I replied, willing myself not to smile.

Maddi glanced at her kitten. She shook her head. "No, I need a dog just like Fay."

Ben and Tamara laughed.

"Looks like you've got a budding search and rescue girl," I said.

Ben looked serious. "I mean it. We're going to help."

"We'll volunteer," Tamara added. "Maddi will grow up understanding the importance of helping others."

"If you decide to get a rescue dog, call me. I know a great breeder. Gary raises awesome Border collies."

Chapter
Fourteen

Fay and I walked back to our SUV, where I'd parked under an amber light on a tall pole. We'd done our job, and now we could relax. I stopped and removed Fay's SAR vest to let her know that her job was over. That meant it was now time for our good-girl party.

This was a routine we usually go through at the finish of the trail, right after Fay gets her Vienna sausages, but in the excitement, I had forgotten. I held my arms out and snapped my fingers. She leaped straight up—to where she was even with my head—and landed neatly in my arms. I caught her and gave her a big hug.

"You are such a good girl. You did a great job. You found Maddi. You stayed by Maddi. You found a way to get me to Maddi when you couldn't leave her. You're the best dog on the planet, Fayva Bean," I said, calling her by the nickname I had given her as a puppy. "You're my good, good girl."

She grinned at me, her tongue lolling out and her ears slicked back in happiness. She squirmed to get down and then leaned against my legs, looking up at me over her shoulder in a show of affection. I had figured out that this bit of body language was Fay's dog hug.

I bent over and snapped my fingers. She sprang up on my back, turning to watch everyone as they clapped. She wagged her tail. It was great fun.

I looked back over my shoulder into her alert eyes. When I was Maddi's age, I read a story about the rare and wise fairy dogs of old that came to live with families and keep them safe from harm. Now I know those dogs are real, and I am lucky enough to work with one who does her best to keep everyone's family safe.

When Fay was satisfied with our good-girl party, she jumped off my back and headed for our vehicle.

Now that the excitement was wearing off, I felt the tiredness in my body. It'd been a long, hard search. I opened the tailgate and Fay jumped inside. I set down

my backpack and pulled out a Vienna sausage to give to Fay as a reward for a job well done. I opened a bottle of water and, sitting on the tailgate, took a long drink.

I felt a poke on my arm and looked over to see Fay's bright eyes watching me. Most dogs would be piled up in the back of the SUV, ready for a long nap on the ride home after so many hours of work. Not Fay. She had her Frisbee in her mouth. She poked me again. Message clear. Let's play.

She jumped off the tailgate and stood in front of me, anticipation in her eyes. I reached for her Frisbee. She yanked it away before I could touch it. We did this several times, and her eyes got brighter. She loved to prove that the dog is faster than the hand. I laughed, grabbing for the Frisbee.

Frisbee isn't something I trained Fay to do. She trained me. And she always makes me work for it. She likes to play after a long day's adventure and a successful find. It's another reward for a job well done.

When I finally got the Frisbee away from her, she took off running. I threw it long and high into the glow of a nearby street light. She sailed into the air and snapped it neatly with her teeth.

It made me laugh every time to see her floating through the air as if in slow motion, her legs hanging down, the Frisbee in her mouth, the funny way she splayed out her toes to land. Then she'd hit the ground running, and we'd start the process all over again.

She quickly drew an audience. People gathered to watch her fly through the air after her Frisbee. They clapped and cheered her on to greater leaps. She enjoyed the attention. Her jumps became more elaborate with flips and turns in the air as the applause increased.

As I played Frisbee with Fay, I realized how lucky people are to have these incredible creatures called dogs to share the world with us. I'm particularly lucky to have a small black-and-white one for a friend and partner. Every day my love and admiration for her grows. And so does my trust.

Hearing my cell phone ding, I pulled it out of my pocket. When I flipped it open, a text message glowed in the darkness.

STAND BY. POSSIBLE SEARCH. DETAILS TO FOLLOW.

"Load up," I told Fay. "Time to go." She sailed neatly into the back of the SUV, dropping her Frisbee as she jumped in her seat.

"Are you ready?" I asked as I slammed the tailgate.

She pricked her ears and cocked her head to the side as if to say, "I'm always ready."

I smiled. "Faith in Fay."

Border Collie Breed Characteristics

Adult Border collies are medium-sized dogs weighing from thirty to fifty-five pounds. They are working dogs and are considered the premier herding breed. Highly intelligent and extremely energetic, they require more exercise than a walk around the block on-lead. They thrive with room to run and a job to do. They will herd anything that moves: objects, other animals, and people.

When considering a Border collie for your home, it is best to have mature, well-behaved children, since these workaholic dogs' herding instincts run deep. They love their families, but can be standoffish with strangers. They are seasonal shedders. Well-socialized, well-trained Border collies are a joy to be around, but owning and teaching them requires lots and lots of time. This is not a dog that can be put in the backyard and left to its own devices. These quick-thinking and fanatically work-minded dogs are bred for and enjoy endless hours of sprinting, stopping, and focusing, which serve to make them top-of-the-line SAR dogs. They are good sport dogs for play and show, such as agility, flyball, Frisbee, and dock diving.

These characteristics make them unsuitable for most homes as just a pet. If you have small children in your household or spend many hours a day away from home with no time for intensive exercise, select a dog more suited to your lifestyle. There is a wealth of information online to assist you in finding the dog of your dreams. Don't forget to check with your local shelters and give an adult dog a second chance.

Visit www.nasar.org to find a Search and Rescue group in your neighborhood. Volunteer your time and resources to this life-changing cause.

About the Authors

Sherri   Paula   Fay

Sherri Watson was born and raised in the small town of Cyril, Oklahoma, where old-fashioned values and love abounded. Most of her youth was spent on a tractor or climbing haystacks in the huge barn. The devoted mother of two wonderful boys, Brandon and Bradon, Sherri exercised her huge capacity to love as she raised kids, puppies, foals, and calves alongside the love of her life, her late husband Gary.

Shortly after Gary was killed in an accident, the family Border collies, Lexi and Sam, also passed away. Not wanting Gary's or Sam and Lexi's legacy to die with them, Sherri set out to write a story about the daughter of her much-loved collies—Fay.

Paula Abney was born in North Georgia. Her youth was spent on the back of a horse exploring the countryside with a good dog at her heels, which continued after she became the mother of two daughters, Mecca and Jessie. An avid outdoor person and dog lover, Paula felt an intense desire to "give something back," and after a chance meeting with Sherri and the adoption of Fay, she transitioned easily into search and rescue work.

Fay, a dog with more personality in a tail hair than most people have, started search training as a puppy and was mission ready in trailing by two years old. She loves her job. Fay's other passions include swimming, playing Frisbee, playing basketball (or any kind of ball), riding anything that moves, herding anything that moves, whitewater rafting, and exploring. When bored, she invents new games to keep herself occupied. She loves playing at the beach with Paula's grandkids and going wherever Paula goes.

After coauthoring *The Ultimate Dream* with another friend, Sherri approached Paula with her idea of *Faith in Fay* as the first book in a children's series. Given the important nature of the content, *Faith in Fay* was written not only with an eye to keep the story true to life, but also to spread awareness of volunteer K-9 Search & Rescue teams and to help educate readers about dog breeds, their characteristics, and the positive ways dogs impact our lives. They sincerely hope that this book is as uplifting and enjoyable to the readers as it was for the writers.